the CRiTTeR club

Liz's Perfect Painting

by Callie Barkley 🐾 illustrated by Tracy Bishop

LITTLE SIMON
New York London Toronto Sydney New Delhi

LITTLE SIMON

An imprint of Simon & Schuster Children's Publishing Division

1230 Avenue of the Americas, New York, New York 10020

First Little Simon paperback edition March 2024

Copyright © 2024 by Simon & Schuster, LLC. All rights reserved, including the right of reproduction in whole or in part in any form.

LITTLE SIMON is a registered trademark of Simon & Schuster, LLC, and associated colophon is a trademark of Simon & Schuster, LLC.

Simon & Schuster: Celebrating 100 Years of Publishing in 2024

For information about special discounts for bulk purchases, please contact Simon & Schuster Special Sales at 1-866-506-1949 or business@simonandschuster.com.

The Simon & Schuster Speakers Bureau can bring authors to your live event. For more information or to book an event contact the Simon & Schuster Speakers Bureau at 1-866-248-3049 or visit our website at www.simonspeakers.com.

Designed by Sarah Richards Taylor

Manufactured in the United States of America 0124 LAK

10 9 8 7 6 5 4 3 2 1

Cataloging-in-Publication Data for this title is available from the Library of Congress.

ISBN 978-1-6659-5322-1 (hc)

ISBN 978-1-6659-5321-4 (pbk)

ISBN 978-1-6659-5323-8 (ebook)

Table of Contents

Chapter 1

Artist in the Attic

Up in the attic, Liz Jenkins was trying to do two things at once.

"Reggie, no!" Liz called to her ferret. "Leave it."

Liz was making sure her pet didn't get into any trouble. Reggie backed out of a dusty box with a sock on his head. He shook it off.

Reggie ran across the room and dug in his basket of ferret toys.

Liz was trying hard to finish up a painting. The attic was now her art studio. Liz's parents had helped her clear some space. They set up her easel. They found a small table and a chair in storage. They even cleared an old bookcase that was perfect for holding Liz's art supplies.

And she had *a lot* of art supplies. Watercolors. Paintbrushes. Colored pencils. Paper for collages. Pens and ink. Seeing her supplies all together made Liz want to jump with joy.

Today Liz was painting with acrylic paint. It was a floral still life for her Aunt Biz. Her real name was Elizabeth—just like Liz's! But everyone called her Biz.

Aunt Biz's birthday was coming up. And she loved flowers, especially

sunflowers. So far, Liz thought
the vase she was painting looked
pretty good. But not
the flower petals.

"What do you
think?" Liz asked
Reggie.

She picked Reggie up. "Is it weird that I talk to you?"

Nah, thought Liz. She knew her best friends Amy, Ellie, and Marion would agree too. They all loved animals. That's why the four of them had created The Critter Club, set up inside their friend Ms. Sullivan's barn. They cared for strays, found lost pets, did some pet-sitting, and even nursed injured wild animals.

And they talked to animals all the time.

"Liz!" her dad's voice called out from the bottom of the attic steps. Reggie jumped off Liz's lap. He ran over to the top of the stairs. Liz followed.

Down below, Mr. Jenkins waved up at them. "Sunday dinner in ten minutes!"

Liz scrunched her face. "Okay," she replied.

Her dad came up the stairs. "What's the matter?" he asked Liz.

He gave Reggie a little pat too. "You love black bean burger night."

She pointed to her painting. "I'm just trying to fix these petals. I can't get them right."

Her dad put his hand on her shoulder. "Liz, that's beautiful. I think you've gotten the flower's essence."

Liz sighed. "But it doesn't look like the real petals. I want to get it *exactly*."

Her dad nodded. "I understand," he said. "It's not living up to your expectations. But hey, sometimes

the unexpected can be even better."

Liz was quiet for a few moments. "I guess," she said with a shrug. But deep down, Liz knew there had to be a way to fix those flowers.

chapter 2

The Best Monday

Monday was Liz's favorite day of the week at school. Art day! They had art right before lunch. Mrs. Sienna led the class down the hall to the art room.

Liz took the seat next to Marion. Amy and Ellie sat across from them at the same table.

"Hey, guess what!" Amy whispered. "A family at Mom's clinic asked about pet-sitters. They're going out of town and need someone to watch their pet."

Amy's mom was Dr. Melanie Purvis, a veterinarian. She had helped the girls get The Critter Club started.

Ellie did a happy dance in her chair. "Oooh, what did your mom say?" she asked.

Amy put her hands on her hips. "She told the family about The Critter Club, of course!" she replied.

"I'll make up a schedule for us," Marion said. She loved to do the organizing for the club.

"You didn't say what kind of pet," Liz pointed out.

"Oh, I forgot! Her name is Cleo,"

Amy said. She smiled at Liz. "She's a ferret!"

Ellie laughed. "Liz's favorite!" she cried. They all knew Liz loved unusual animals.

The more unusual, the better. And of course, she had a soft spot for ferrets.

"Ooh! I have toys Reggie doesn't play with anymore," Liz told Amy.

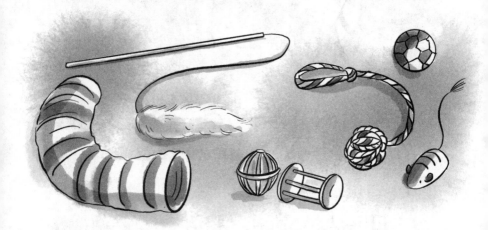

"And ferret treats, too. I can bring them for Cleo, if her family says it's okay."

Just then Mrs. Cummings, the art teacher, asked for the class's attention.

"Today we're going to finish up our cut-paper projects," Mrs. Cummings said. "But first, I have some news."

She told them about a local artist named Toni Su. She was a painter having a show at a nearby art gallery. "She got her start when another artist included her art in their show. Now, she would like to feature some student art in *her* show."

"If you like to paint, please bring in your best artwork next Monday. Toni Su will be here! You can show her your paintings. And who knows? Maybe yours will be chosen for her gallery show."

This was almost too much for Liz to even hope for! The idea of her own art, displayed in a real gallery? Liz realized her mouth was hanging open in awe, and she closed it.

"I know someone who likes to paint," Marion whispered, smiling at Liz.

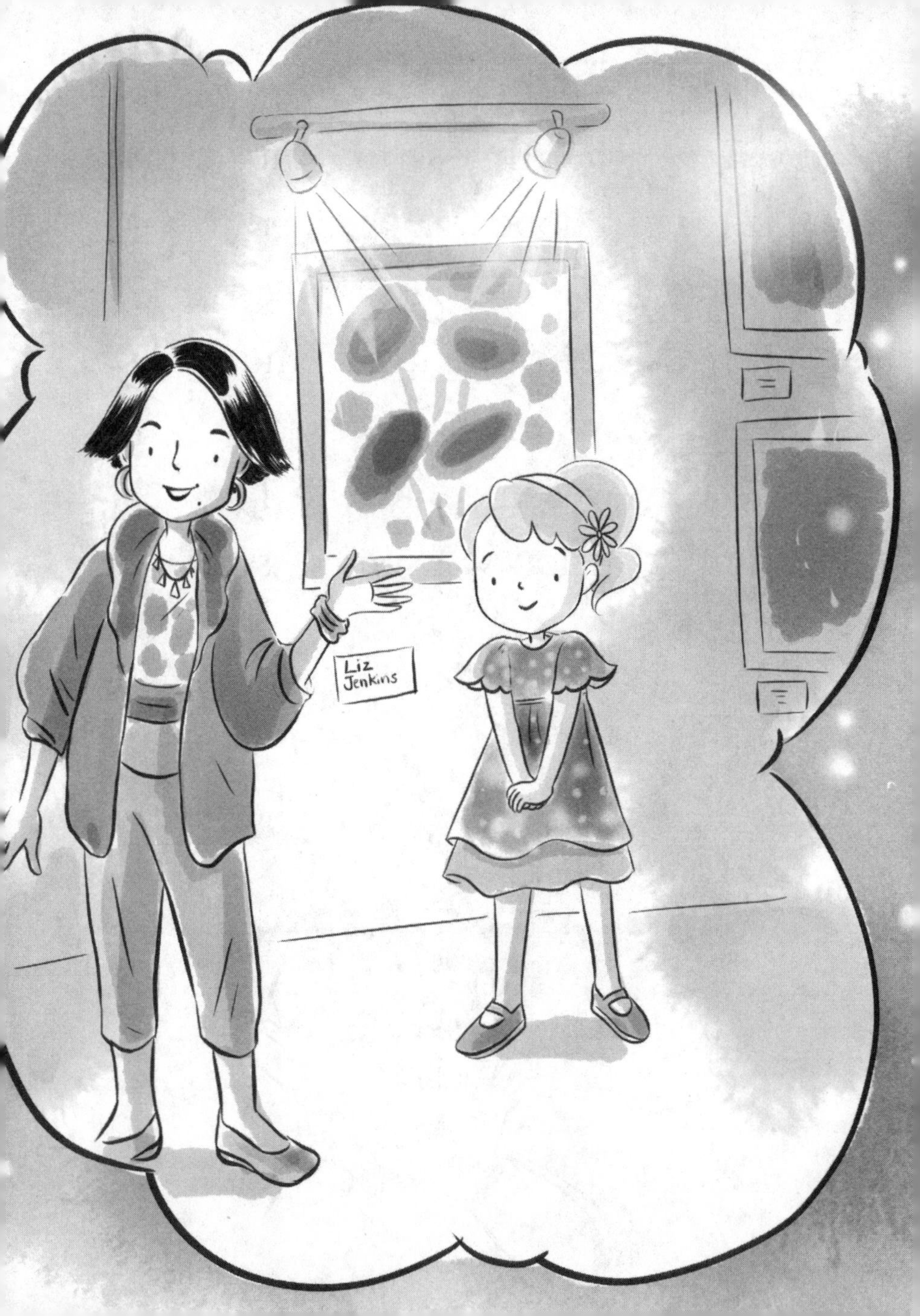
Liz
Jenkins

Chapter 3

Liz Makes Plans

"Best day ever!" Liz shouted on the ride home.

She told her mom about the ferret coming to stay at The Critter Club. And she told her about the artist looking for student paintings.

"Art and ferrets!" her mom said. "Two of your favorite things!"

At home, Liz went straight to the bin of Reggie's toys. Some toys were Reggie's favorites. You could tell by how worn out they were. Other toys looked almost brand-new. Reggie hadn't been interested in them. *But maybe Cleo would be!* Liz thought.

Liz took a reusable tote from the kitchen. She picked out some of

the new-looking toys: a chew toy in the shape of a pretzel, a clear ball with colorful bells, a fabric hideaway house with crinkle paper sewn inside. When Reggie ducked into it, the noise had startled him. Liz also added a pouch of Reggie's favorite ferret treats.

Then she climbed up to her art studio. On the easel sat her unfinished painting for Aunt Biz. Good thing her birthday wasn't for a few weeks, because now Liz had another painting to focus on. What was she going to paint to show Toni Su?

Liz let Reggie out of his cage. She put his harness and leash on him, so she could coax him out of any mess he got into. Then she got out her sketchbook and did a few quick sketches. She sketched the plant by the attic window. *I could do another still life.* Except her flower still life wasn't working out.

Liz sketched a landscape of the fields behind Ms. Sullivan's barn. She turned the page and did a sketch of the seashore.

Then Liz looked over at Reggie. He was inside an old laundry basket. Reggie leaned on the rim, trying to climb out. Instead, the basket tipped and then flopped over on top of him.

"I wish I could paint you," Liz said to Reggie, laughing, "except

no way would you stand still."

Liz was so curious to see what Cleo was like. Could she be as curious and energetic as Reggie?

Cleo's New Friends

On Tuesday after school, Liz's dad dropped her off at The Critter Club. She had the tote full of ferret toys and treats. She couldn't wait to meet Cleo!

Marion, Amy, and Ellie were already there. They were sitting very quietly.

A ferret was curled up on Ellie's lap, fast asleep. *Asleep!* Liz had never seen Reggie asleep outside his cage. Ellie pet Cleo gently along her

back. "Amy and I got here first and let her out," Ellie said. She pointed at the ferret cage Cleo's owner had brought over.

"She ran around for a few minutes," Amy said. "Then she climbed into Ellie's lap and . . ."

"Awww," said Liz. "Maybe she's missing her family." Liz explained that ferrets were social animals. They loved to have company.

Liz sat down next to Ellie and Cleo. She started taking the toys out of her tote. The clear ball jingled as she set it down. Cleo's ears perked up and she lifted her head.

Cleo hopped off Ellie's lap. She sniffed at the ball. Then she batted it. *Jingle, jangle!* Cleo hopped on the ball. It rolled out from under her.

Liz grabbed the ball and rolled it to Marion. Cleo chased after it.

Marion rolled it to Ellie. Ellie rolled it to Amy. Cleo pounced on the ball and rolled over on her back, hugging it. The girls all laughed.

Cleo liked the other toys, too, but not as much as the ball. Then Cleo sniffed inside the tote bag. She pulled out the bag of treats.

Now Cleo was acting more like Reggie! He could always sniff out food.

"Okay, just one," said Liz. "Too many treats aren't good for you."

Liz tossed Cleo a ferret treat. Cleo caught it in her mouth and gobbled it up.

Just then Ms. Sullivan appeared in the doorway. She had her dog, Rufus, on a leash. Ms. Sullivan had been on Cleo duty that morning. "I thought I'd bring Rufus to meet her," she said to the girls.

Ms. Sullivan led Rufus over to say hello to Cleo. They sniffed each other's noses. Then gentle Rufus lay down on his belly. He let Cleo sniff his paws and ears. Cleo started climbing all over him. Rufus did not seem to mind one bit.

"Good boy, Rufus," said Amy.
"What a good host."

Cleo did seem to feel right at home. "We should try to spend a lot of time with her," Liz said. "Ferrets don't like to be in their cages a lot."

"That reminds me," said Ms. Sullivan. "Rufus and I will be away this weekend at my friend's wedding."

Ellie squealed. "Oooh, I love weddings!" she cried. Once Ellie had been a flower girl at her cousin Hailey's wedding.

Ms. Sullivan continued. "I won't

be here with Cleo on Saturday or Sunday. Might one of you take her home for the weekend?"

Liz's hand shot up into the air. "I will!" she cried.

Chapter 5

The Pet-Sitter Who Also Paints

Liz's mom and dad agreed to have a guest ferret for the weekend, but it took some convincing.

"Are you sure Cleo and Reggie will get along?" her mom asked.

"Am I *sure*?" Liz said. "Well, no." Cleo hadn't been shy, though, so Liz thought it would be okay.

"Where will Cleo sleep?" asked her dad. "Can she share Reggie's cage?"

Liz shook her head. "No, she'll need her own," she replied. "We'll have to bring it over from The Critter Club."

It was a big cage and a big hassle. But in the end, Liz's parents knew Cleo couldn't be left alone all weekend. And Liz *did* know a lot about ferrets. It made sense.

 On Saturday morning, Liz's parents picked her up from Marion's house

after their weekly sleepover. Then they drove straight to the barn to pick up Cleo. They took apart her cage and stacked the pieces in the back of their minivan.

They drove across Santa Vista.

Cleo sat in Liz's lap, secure in a special harness. Liz opened the window so Cleo could sniff the air.

When they got home, Liz carried Cleo up to the art studio. "Welcome!" she said.

Inside his cage, Reggie stuck his nose through an opening. *Sniff,*

sniff. He spun around twice, then sniffed again. He made a little happy noise, like the clucking of a chicken.

Meanwhile, Liz's parents brought in the cage pieces.

"Listen!" Liz said to them. "Reggie is dooking. That's the noise he's making. He's excited to meet Cleo!"

Liz's mom chuckled. "That's better than hissing. Right?"

"Definitely!" Liz replied.

They set up Cleo's cage close to Reggie's. But not *too* close.

"This will give them their own space," Liz said. "They can get used to each other's scent."

Liz decided to stay in the art studio with them. She didn't want to leave them alone, and she needed

to get started on her painting. She had to bring it to school on Monday!

Liz had been thinking about what to paint all week. Finally, she decided, *I'm going to paint the lake!*

Her family's cabin at Marigold Lake was her favorite place in the world, and it was so beautiful. The sun rising over the pine trees. The geese on the glassy water. The red canoe tied up at the end of the dock. Liz could see it so clearly in her mind's eye.

Liz had spent many summer days on that dock. Amy, Marion, and Ellie sometimes came along for a weekend too. When Liz was there, she felt peaceful and happy.

If she did a good job, just looking at her painting would make her happy.

And maybe Toni Su, too!

Liz put a new canvas on the easel. She got out her brushes and paints. She took a deep breath . . . and she began to paint.

Chapter 6

Liz's Daydream

By bedtime, Liz had painted the water and a sky dotted with clouds.

"Not bad, huh?" she asked Reggie and Cleo.

Liz still had a lot of work to do, like painting cloud reflections in the water. That would be hard to get right.

Reggie was sniffing around the latch of his cage. That was Reggie-speak for, *Can I come out and play?* So Liz opened the latch and Reggie darted out. He went straight over to Cleo's cage.

Cleo backed away at first. But

then she inched toward the cage wall. Soon she was sniffing at Reggie between the bars.

Reggie twirled around. He ran to Liz's feet. He ran back to Cleo's cage. Then he made his happy dooking noise again.

Liz took the ferrets out into the backyard. Her big brother, Stewart, had Reggie on a leash. Liz had Cleo on a leash. The ferrets were happy to walk side by side. Stewart hid some balls inside the fabric tunnel. He and Liz let the ferrets go in after them, one from each end.

"They're getting along great!"
Stewart said.

"I think they could be let off their leashes," Liz said. So Liz unclipped Cleo and Stewart unclipped Reggie.

They watched the ferrets invent
a game. Reggie picked up a ball.
He left it at Cleo's side. Then he ran
away.

Cleo picked up the ball. She ran
after Reggie. When she caught up,

she dropped the ball and ran away.

"It's like the opposite of the keep-away game," Stewart said with a laugh.

"Let's call it ferret ball!" Liz decided.

When the ferrets got tired, Liz took them up to the attic. She put them in their cages so she could paint again.

As Liz studied her painting, she smiled. It looked good. Really good!

Liz imagined her painting hanging on a white wall. Lights on the ceiling shone directly at it. Many people stood in front of the painting, just as Liz was doing now. They were talking quietly, nodding and smiling.

What would the painting's label say? "View from the Lake House"? And under that, "Liz Jenkins" and "Acrylic on canvas."

Maybe people would see her art and ask her for more. Maybe they'd hang up her art in their homes!

In his cage, Reggie squeaked one of his squeeze toys. Liz snapped out of her daydream. The painting wasn't even done. She was getting way, way ahead of herself.

But she was proud of her work. It was turning out to be one of her best.

Maybe this one was going to be her perfect painting.

Ferret Games

On Sunday, Liz gave the ferrets breakfast and filled up their water bottles. Then she let them play ferret ball for a little bit. But soon, it was time to finish her painting.

Liz put Reggie back in his cage. Then she placed Cleo and the ball inside her cage.

"Here," Liz told her. "You hold on to that."

Then Liz sat down at her easel. She didn't have much left to do. Mostly she had to fix the cloud reflections on the lake. They had to look just like clouds. But they also had to show the ripples in the water.

Liz opened two paint jars: blue and white. She put some of each on her palette. She started mixing, intent on getting the perfect shade.

She heard a rattling behind her, like Reggie pushing on his door.

"Reggie," Liz said as she turned. "We'll play later—"

She stopped as she laid eyes on the ferret outside the door of his cage.

Wait, no. Reggie was inside his cage. That was Cleo *outside* his door, trying to get in. She had the ball.

Liz's eyes darted to Cleo's cage.

The door was wide open. Ugh! She meant to close it after giving Cleo the ball. But she had totally forgotten!

Liz put down her brush. "Let's get you back in—"

Cleo dropped the ball and darted away. She was trying to continue the game! But from inside the cage, Reggie couldn't chase her.

Instead, Liz was chasing her. "Wait! Cleo, come back."

Cleo scurried behind some boxes. One toppled off another.

"Cleo!"

The ferret jumped onto an old lamp, scratching the lampshade with her nails.

"Hey!"

Cleo ran between Liz's legs and stopped for a second under Liz's easel.

Liz gasped and held her breath. "Careful, Cleo. Don't knock over my painting!"

Cleo sprang up onto Liz's chair. She jumped onto the chair back, then onto the paint shelf. *Phew!* At least now Cleo was too high to knock her painting over.

"Here, Cleo," Liz said gently. "Come on. Jump to me."

Liz held out her arms to catch her.

Cleo looked at Liz, understanding. She inched to the edge of the shelf. Then she sprang forward to Liz.

As she did, Cleo's back legs caught the side of a jar. A jar of blue paint. With the lid still unscrewed.

All at once, Cleo was flying through the air toward Liz. And a blue paint jar was falling right toward Liz's painting.

Splat!

A second later, there was blue

everywhere. Blue dripped off Liz's chair. Blue puddled on the floor. And there were big blue streaks across Liz's landscape.

Liz could hardly bear to look at her easel.

Liz carried Cleo and safely put her back inside the cage. She made sure to close and latch the door.

Then Liz went back to see the damage. The blue paint was straight across the middle of the painting. The cloud reflections on the lake were ruined.

"I was so close!" Liz shouted. So close to having the perfect painting to submit.

She felt tears welling in her eyes.

Liz ran downstairs and out onto the front porch. She sat down on the top step. Fresh air usually helped her calm down. Liz took deep breaths. She tried not to think of the gallery show.

That dream was gone.

The screen door opened. Liz's mom came out. She sat down next to Liz. "Honeybun," she said gently, "what happened?"

Liz couldn't find the words. She lay her head on her mom's shoulder and cried.

Unexpected Art

For once, Liz wasn't happy it was Monday.

Yes, it was art day. But she felt pretty down about her painting. She had scraped off as much of the blue paint as she could, and added shadows and gray clouds to cover up the remaining streaks.

Her painting wasn't what she had pictured. And it was definitely no masterpiece. She hid it inside a brown paper bag, so no one could see it.

At school, she saw Amy, Ellie, and Marion by the lockers. But Liz didn't stop to say hi until *after* she had put the brown bag inside her locker.

When it was time for art, Liz carried her canvas to the art room against her chest, painted side in.

Mrs. Cummings pointed to a side table. "Please place any art submissions here," she said. Liz put hers face down. Then she sat down and tried to forget about it.

That got easier when Mrs. Cummings introduced their guest: the artist, Toni Su! She was already there, sitting by Mrs. Cummings's desk. And she had prepared a presentation of her work.

Mrs. Cummings turned down the lights. Ms. Su clicked to her first slide.

Liz gasped. The whiteboard was filled with an explosion of colors and shapes. It wasn't so much a painting of a thing or a place.

To Liz, it looked like a painting of a feeling. It was not at all like the art Liz made.

"I call this work 'Celebration,'" Ms. Su said.

Liz listened intently. She was captivated as the artist clicked through slide after slide. Each painting was so unique. Different colors, different amounts of white space, different brushstrokes. Some looked very calm and swirly, and others looked very energetic with lots of straight lines.

Twenty minutes passed in what felt like a blink. Mrs. Cummings turned the lights up.

"And now," said Ms. Su, "I can't wait to see *your* work!"

During the slideshow, Mrs. Cummings had put out all the submissions on easels. Ms. Su and the whole class could walk around and see them all.

Liz avoided her own painting. But she did love seeing everyone else's! Some had painted still lifes. Some painted portraits: one of a dog, one of a grandparent. Some had even done abstract pieces.

"It's hard to choose just one for my show," Ms. Su said. "They all deserve a gallery show."

Mrs. Cummings flashed a smile. "Actually, they will *all* be hung up in the school lobby next week," she said. "That will be our school gallery. All the students will be able to go see them."

Liz shrugged. *That's nice,* she thought. So even if Ms. Su didn't choose her art, it would be displayed. Liz went over to her painting and took another look. Her eye went right to the cover-up area. But actually, it was not bad. She did put a lot of work into it.

Liz knew she should be proud of that.

Chapter 9

A Huge Surprise

After school, Liz brought Cleo back to The Critter Club. Her owners would pick her up after dinnertime.

Amy, Marion, and Ellie helped reassemble Cleo's cage. Then Liz showed them how to play ferret ball. The girls took turns tossing and fetching the ball.

"Is everything okay, Liz?" Marion suddenly asked. "You've been really quiet today."

"Oh, umm . . . ," Liz said, but then Cleo scampered toward her and ran in circles around her feet.

"Aww. Liz is just sad to see Cleo leave!" Ellie said.

Liz smiled weakly and nodded. She couldn't be mad at Cleo. The ruined painting had been an accident. Still, Liz felt too sad to tell her friends what had happened.

She gave Cleo one last goodbye snuggle. Then she put Cleo in the cage and placed the ball inside too. "It's a present from me and Reggie," she said.

"Liz!" her dad called from the kitchen. "Phone call for you!"

Liz had just gotten back from The Critter Club. It might be Cleo's owners calling. Did she forget to give back something of Cleo's?

"Liz?" said the voice on the other end of the phone. "This is Toni Su."

"Oh," said Liz. She couldn't think of anything else to say.

"I love your painting of the lake," Ms. Su told Liz. "So I'm calling to ask you, can I put it in my show next weekend?"

Now Liz *really* didn't know what to say. How could this be? Her painting? But really? How?

"Liz?" said Ms. Su. "Are you there?"

Liz cleared her throat. "Yes! Yes, I'm here!" she squeaked.

"I'm sorry. I–I can't believe this. My painting wasn't exactly perfect."

Ms. Su laughed. "Oh, my artwork is never perfect either. But you know what? That's my favorite thing about being an artist. You're always changing, and growing,

and getting better every day."

A big smile spread across Liz's face. After everything that happened, a professional artist had noticed *her* artwork! She couldn't wait to tell her best friends.

Liz Jenkins, Artist

The next weekend was the night of the big art show! Liz dressed up in a colorful long skirt.

When Liz and her family arrived, there were already a lot of people inside. Liz waved at Ms. Su, but she was busy talking to a group of grown-ups.

"Wow!" Liz exclaimed. They stood in front of one of Ms. Su's paintings. The canvas was huge! In fact, all the paintings were huge. Now Liz was even more in awe. She could see how thickly the paint was layered on.

They moved down the wall of large paintings. Liz stopped in front of a painting called "Sunflower." The canvas was covered in crisscross brushstrokes.

The painting looked nothing like a flower, but it still reminded Liz of a bright, happy sunflower. She thought of the sunflowers she was painting for her Aunt Biz. *Maybe the petals don't need to look perfectly realistic after all,* she thought.

A part of Liz wanted to go home and finish painting the sunflowers right away. But there was one more painting to look at first.

"There's mine!" Liz cried. She led her family to a smaller work at the end of the wall. It was Liz's landscape, hung up just like Toni Su's artwork.

And underneath was a label!

"Elizabeth Jenkins," her dad read aloud. "Artist from Santa Vista Elementary."

"Way to go!" Stewart said, grinning.

Liz's mom insisted on taking a family picture in front of the painting. Liz wasn't embarrassed, though. She felt proud!

Someone tapped Liz on the shoulder. It was Amy, with Marion and Ellie. "Congratulations!" Amy cried.

Ellie grabbed Liz's arm. "Your painting looks even more amazing here, in a real art gallery!"

"How did you paint something so beautiful?" Marion asked.

Liz smiled. "With a little help from Cleo," she said.

Her friends looked at her, confused.

"I'll tell you all about it later," Liz said, smiling. For now, Liz wanted to enjoy her very first gallery show—and her perfectly imperfect painting.